Dear Parent:
Your child's love of reading starts here!

Every child learns to read in a different way and at his or her own speed. Some go back and forth between reading levels and read favorite books again and again. Others read through each level in order. You can help your young reader improve and become more confident by encouraging his or her own interests and abilities. From books your child reads with you to the first books he or she reads alone, there are I Can Read Books for every stage of reading:

SHARED READING
Basic language, word repetition, and whimsical illustrations, ideal for sharing with your emergent reader

BEGINNING READING
Short sentences, familiar words, and simple concepts for children eager to read on their own

READING WITH HELP
Engaging stories, longer sentences, and language play for developing readers

READING ALONE
Complex plots, challenging vocabulary, and high-interest topics for the independent reader

ADVANCED READING
Short paragraphs, chapters, and exciting themes for the perfect bridge to chapter books

I Can Read Books have introduced children to the joy of reading since 1957. Featuring award-winning authors and illustrators and a fabulous cast of beloved characters, I Can Read Books set the standard for beginning readers.

A lifetime of discovery begins with the magical words "I Can Read!"

Visit www.icanread.com for information
on enriching your child's reading experience.

For my friend and illustrator
extraordinaire, Pat Schories!
—A.S.C.

ISBN 978-0-545-32165-5

30 29

22/0

Printed in the U.S.A.

40

First Scholastic printing, November 2010

Biscuit Meets the Class Pet

story by ALYSSA SATIN CAPUCILLI

pictures by PAT SCHORIES

SCHOLASTIC INC.
New York Toronto London Auckland
Sydney Mexico City New Delhi Hong Kong

Here, Biscuit.

Come meet Nibbles!

Woof, woof!

This is Nibbles.

Nibbles is our class pet.

Nibbles is here for a visit.

Woof, woof!

Hop, hop!

Look, Biscuit!

Nibbles found your bone.

Woof, woof!

Hop, hop!

Nibbles found your ball.

Woof, woof!

Hop, hop!

Nibbles found your bed, too!

Woof!

Silly puppy!

No tugging.

Stay here, Biscuit.
I will get a snack
for Nibbles.

Woof, woof!

Hop, hop!

Woof!

Hop, hop!

Woof!

Hop, hop!

Woof, woof! Woof, woof!

Hop!

Oh no, Biscuit!

Where is Nibbles?

Woof, woof!

We must find him.

Woof, woof!

Nibbles is not under the table.

Woof, woof!

Nibbles is not on the chair.

Woof, woof!

Where can Nibbles be?

Woof, woof!
Sweet puppy!

Nibbles found your bone
and your ball
and your bed!

Woof, woof!
And you found Nibbles.
Woof!